THE CHRISTMAS THAT SANTA SHAVED OFF HIS BEARD

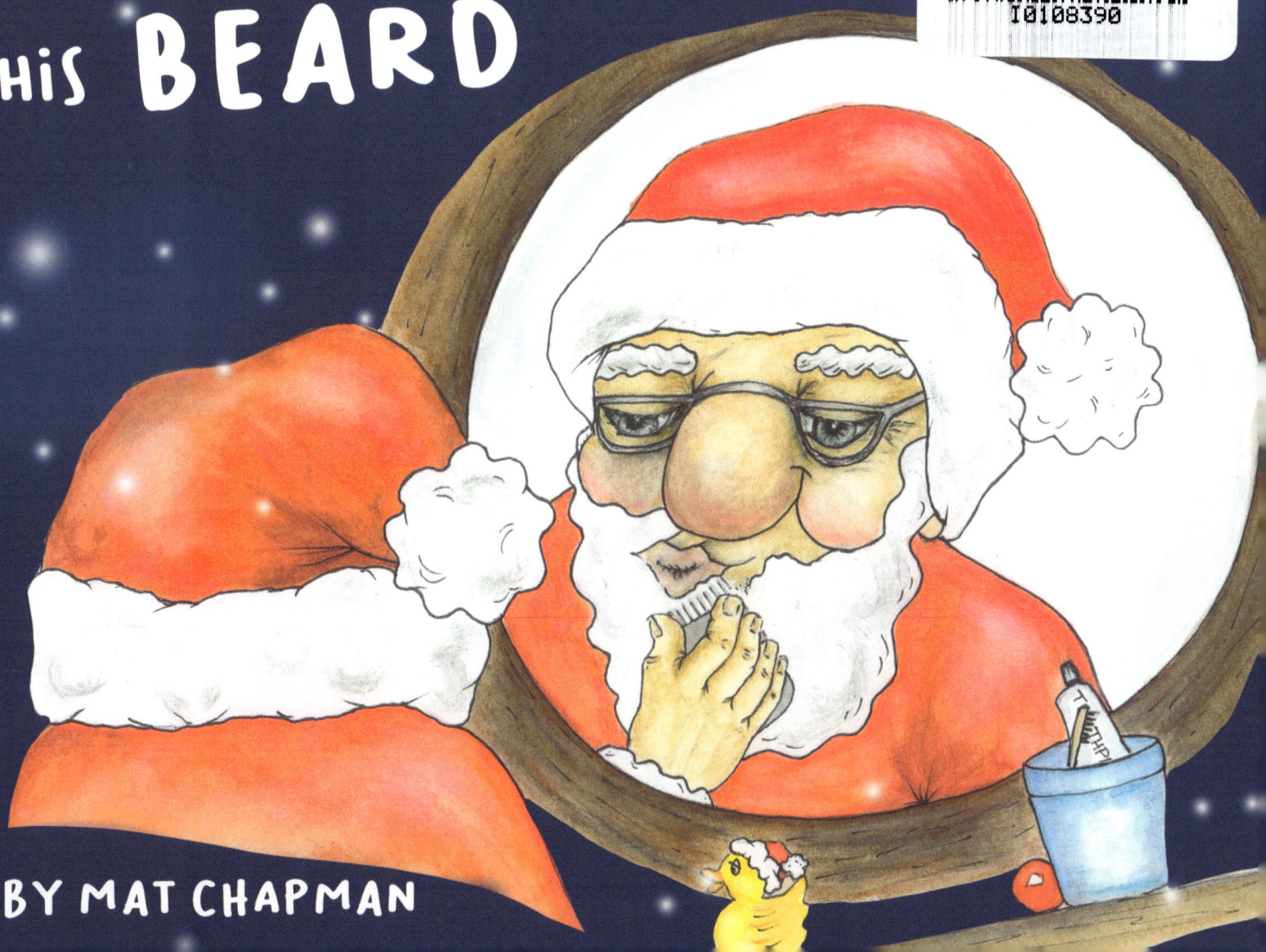

BY MAT CHAPMAN

First published 2024
by Rowanvale Books Ltd
The Gate
Keppoch Street
Roath
Cardiff
CF24 3JW
www.rowanvalebooks.com
Library Cataloguing in Publication Data.
A catalogue record for this book is available from the British Library.

To Luke and Amy. I wish I had written this when you were small enough to sit on my knee and read this together!

To my goddaughter, Boni. I hope this becomes a favourite book for you x

Looking back now, it's
hard to **believe**

the events that
unfolded one
Christmas Eve.

SANTAS HOUSE

It was the Christmas that went a little bit WEiRD,
the Christmas that Santa Shaved off his beard!

No one knows
why he decided to
trim

all the hair from his
head and whiskers

from **chin,**

but from that very first snip it wasn't that **long**

'til things started to go a little bit **wrong**.

Without all his hair, his hat was too big,

and to keep it on
tight, he needed a
Wig.

The night had started to get a bit WEiRD,
all because Santa had Shaved off his beard!

As he readied the Sleigh, out by the **Shed,**

Santa noticed that Rudolph's nose wasn't **red.**

He stared open-
mouthed through a
flurry of **Snow**

as poor Rudolph's
tail started to
glow!

In order to get the flight **underway**,
he attached Rudolph **backwards** onto the **Sleigh**.

Then, as the night began to get **Colder**,
Rudolph took off looking over his **Shoulder!**

Santa in a wig was a very strange **Sight**,
especially with Rudolph in reverse **flight**.

The night was getting really quite WEiRD,
and all because Santa had shaved off his beard!

Once on the roofs,
it was time to
get **busy**,
but he found he
couldn't quite
fit down the
chimneys!

He started to
panic, then he
started to
worry;

he knew that he
really needed to
hurry.

He started leaving
presents anywhere
that he **could**,
without checking his
list for naughty or
good.

Some by the bins, some by front **doors**,
some in greenhouses, some in log **stores.**

There were even some presents
left out on front **paths**;

wrapping paper glistened in
the light of the **stars**.

There had never been a Christmas so WEiRD,
as the one when Santa Shaved off his beard!

Even though he found a few front doors **unlocked**,

he then put the wrong presents in the wrong **socks!**

Little girls ended up getting Dad's tools,

whilst the boys received Mum's sparkly jewels.

Dad was gifted a pretty, pink dress,

while Mum was left a brand-new train set.

Even the pets didn't miss **out**-
the cat got a bone, and the dog got a **mouse.**

It was certainly a Christmas not to **forget**-
the goldfish was left a backgammon **set!**

That Christmas really was incredibly WEiRD,

the one when Santa Shaved off his beard!

Still to come was the biggest Surprise:
Santa didn't like the taste of mince pies.

In fact, he found he
could no longer eat

cookies or biscuits
or other sweet
treats.

Eating the treats had always been **easy**,

but just thinking of them made him feel **queasy**.

They made him feel as sick as a **parrot**,

so the only thing left was to eat Rudolph's **carrots**!

With his belly quite full, it was time to head **back**,
the reindeer worn out and an empty toy **Sack**.

As he headed home, he thought how **Strange**
the night had been—Since he'd had a **Shave**.

He thought of all the things
that had gone **bad**;

it was the weirdest
Christmas that he'd
ever **had**.

In fact, because it had been so **weird**,
he vowed never again to shave off his **beard**!

Author Profile

I grew up in the small seaside town of Broadstairs, in Kent, where I developed a deep love of the sea and being at the beach. In turn, I became a keen surfer and have enjoyed trips all over the world chasing waves. After working in the gas industry for nearly 30 years, my family and I moved to Wales, where we settled in a peaceful and friendly seaside village, and life took on a more gentle pace. As a child, I was a ferocious reader and always dreamt that one day I would write my own books. Finally, I have taken the plunge, and I hope you enjoy my first attempt, The Christmas That Santa Shaved off His Beard.

What Did You Think of The Christmas That Santa Shaved off His Beard?

A big thank you for purchasing this book. It means a lot that you chose this book specifically from such a wide range on offer. I do hope you enjoyed it.

Book reviews are incredibly important for an author. All feedback helps them improve their writing for future projects and for developing this edition. If you are able to spare a few minutes to post a review on Amazon, that would be much appreciated.

Publisher Information

rowanvale books

Rowanvale Books provides publishing services to independent authors, writers and poets all over the globe. We deliver a personal, honest and efficient service that allows authors to see their work published, while remaining in control of the process and retaining their creativity. By making publishing services available to authors in a cost-effective and ethical way, we at Rowanvale Books hope to ensure that the local, national and international community benefits from a steady stream of good quality literature.

For more information about us, our authors or our publications, please get in touch.
www.rowanvalebooks.com
info@rowanvalebooks.com

www.ingramcontent.com/pod-product-compliance
Lightning Source LLC
Chambersburg PA
CBHW041556040426
42447CB00002B/189